ALL OR SOMETHING

CAROLINA REBELS
BOOK 9

LINDSAY PAIGE

First edition: October 2023
Library of Congress Cataloging-in-Publication Data

Paige, Lindsay
All or Something (a Carolina Rebels novella) – 1st ed
ISBN: 978-1-962174-01-5

CHAPTER 1

SERGEY

M y focus is so intent on giving my studio apartment a good scrubbing that I nearly miss the banging on my door and someone shouting from the other side. With an irritated sigh, I storm over and fling it open.

"Finally. What are you doing in here?" Scotty asks as he steps inside.

"Cleaning."

His nose wrinkles as the smell of bleach hits him. "Why?"

"Because. Why are you here?" I ask, grabbing him a beer and tossing it his way.

"I was nearby and Sylvie called. Long story short, we wanted to invite you over today. The girls, particularly, are anxious to see you. You haven't been over in a bit."

"I'll think about it." Ignoring him, I return to my cleaning. I'm almost done.

"What? Are you too busy cleaning? That's what you want me to tell my girls? Take a break. The dust will be here tomorrow."

I appreciate Scotty's friendship. He doesn't understand

what it has done for me, what his family has done for me, during this time without my wife who isn't my wife.

"Serge," he starts, and I can tell he's about to start in on me.

But a knock interrupts him before he can. I huff, even more irritated now. If another teammate is on the other side of this door, I'm going to punch someone. When I open it, my heart stops and falls to the ground. It can't be. The cleaning products must have me hallucinating.

"Galina," I breathe. Could she really be here? My wife stands with her luggage next to her. "What are you doing here?"

"Either give me a baby or give me a divorce," she demands, her tone full of annoyance.

Behind me, Scotty chokes on his beer and coughs. Right. He's here. At least that confirms Galina really is standing in my doorway.

Galina peers around me. "Oh, I'm sorry, Sergey. I didn't realize you had company. Hello," she says to him with a tight smile and a small wave.

He waves and says hi back. His eyes bounce back and forth between us. Not knowing what exactly to do, I grab her luggage and bring it inside.

"Galina, this is my teammate, Scotty. Scott, this is my wife, Galina."

His eyes nearly burst as he reaches out to shake her hand. "Nice to meet you. We'll have to get together at some point, so you can meet my wife and kids." He clears his throat. "I'll talk to you later, Serge." He slaps me on the back as he walks past me and lets himself out.

"So, this is your place?" she says a moment after he's gone as she gives my apartment a once-over.

"I'm sorry." I know she is used to grandeur and fancy things. This apartment doesn't even have a proper bedroom.

Galina turns to face me with a smile. "I like it. Simple."

She glances down at her luggage. "Where should I put my things?"

"You're staying here?"

She raises an eyebrow at me. "You want me to stay at a hotel?"

"Well, there's only one bed."

She waves a hand at the couch and plops down on it. "There's also a couch. Come sit; we have much to catch up on."

"Yes. You show up out of nowhere and demand a baby or a divorce? What the hell?" I take a seat next to her. It's crazy that she's actually here. My brain hasn't begun to wrap around the complications of this yet. It's so odd to see her after so long without her. My eyes drink her in over and over, looking for what's the same and what's different. "You look amazing, Galina."

She pushes her hair back behind her ear. It's an almost shy move, which is a bit of a wonderment because there isn't much that is shy about Galina. "You have a beard," she says in response.

I laugh. When she last saw me, I always kept my face clean-shaven. I'm sure it is startling for her to see me like this. "I can shave." Why I'm offering to do such a thing for a wife who is a wife in name only, I don't know. But without a doubt, I'd do it if she wanted me to.

She shakes her head. "I don't want to change you." She looks around again. "How do you like it here? In this state? With this team?"

"Better than the last on both accounts." We do keep in touch. Sparsely, but in touch. "How are you?"

"Good. I actually have a job here in the States now." Galina's shoulders sag as she clasps her hands in her lap. Her entire demeanor changes. It doesn't take a rocket scientist to know she's circling back to her earlier demand.

"I can't take it anymore, Sergey; that's why I came. We're

married, but we're not. Your parents haven't given me a moment's peace since we went our separate ways. We need to resolve this one way or another." She gives me a quick glance, but then focuses on her hands again. "But there is something I must tell you before we go any further." Her breaths have turned shaky. Between that and her words, I brace myself. Something bad is surely coming. "I feel that you have the right to know that...that I was with someone else."

I clutch the edge of the couch cushion. All this time, I remained faithful to our vows, sham of a marriage or not. It's been one of the hardest things I've ever had to do, but I've done it. Yet she was out with someone else. My sense of betrayal is unwarranted, I know, but it's there all the same.

Our parents insisted on pairing us together with a matchmaker all those years ago. While I wasn't thrilled about it, I also didn't mind all that much because I'd always had a crush on Galina. We even hung out some and fooled around a little. Our parents setting us up, to me, meant I might have a real chance with Galina. She'd have to give me the time of day; she'd have to spend more time with me. I always just hoped that by doing so would mean she would like me back and it could grow from there.

But Galina? She was abhorred by the idea of her parents wanting to pick her husband. I could have been a king and she still wouldn't want me. That's how much she hated the idea. She didn't dislike me; she disliked what I represented, and that was enough for her to sever ties with me aside from the occasional text.

But me? I hoped she'd come around. Letting go of that hope was futile. Even now, there's hope. She's here, after all. Seeing her on our wedding day, grumpy and upset, she was still the most beautiful creature to ever walk the earth. That image haunts me frequently.

"We were separated," she says, bringing me back to the present.

"Is that why you demand a divorce? Because of this other person?" I should have tried harder during our time apart to bring us together. I've lost her already.

"No," she says with a shake of her head. Relief fills me. "Have you heard from your parents lately?"

My parents? This is the second time she's mentioned them and I'm not sure why. "No," I reply.

Galina smiles. "Of course you wouldn't. Why bother Mr. Success with the troubles of our fake marriage?" She sighs. "Ever since I moved here, they have it in their heads that I've come to my senses and have come here for you. They keep talking about how I need to step up, perform my wifely duties," her nose scrunches in distaste, "and worst of all, it's apparently time to have a baby. I'm tired of hearing it, Sergey. So, either help me give them a baby or give me a divorce so I can move on with my life."

"Why don't you have a baby with the person you've found?"

She rolls her eyes at me. "Because that would cause more trouble and," she pauses briefly, "he's not the kind of man you want to have a baby with. I'm not with him anymore either."

That makes me want to ask all kinds of questions, but I don't. It doesn't feel like it's my place to ask more. "So divorce or a baby? Those are our only options?" My brows furrow. Those can't be our only options, can they? Does Galina truly think either of those will solve her problems? "You honestly want to raise a baby alone?" The idea makes me cringe. I'll divorce her before it comes to that. I won't allow her to do such a thing and certainly not with my child.

"I just want this to be over with, Sergey," she says with a heavy, defeated sigh.

"I guess I'll see if I can find a lawyer to draw up the paper-work for us." That seems to be the only option remaining. My heart breaks a little at the thought. There's something about

Galina that is hard to let go of. She never wanted to get married, but she did. This is the first time she's asked for an out. How can I not give it to her?

Galina blinks in surprise, as if she wasn't actually expecting me to do as she wanted. I start to stand, deciding to take Scotty up on his offer because a little space from Galina sounds nice right about now. My attraction to her has only grown; it's obvious her stance remains unchanged. I'm stopped in my tracks when Galina reaches out and grabs my wedding band that has slipped out of my shirt, exposing itself when I leaned forward.

"You wear it still?" she breathes in surprise.

As I glance over her, I see that she wears a necklace, but it's of the decorative sort. The ring on her finger is not the band I gave her.

"I take my vows seriously, Galina, even if the marriage isn't."

She releases her hold on my necklace.

"I'm heading out," I say. She's been back in my life less than twenty minutes and I'm already walking away from her. She already has my emotions in a tangled mess. Am I even a man? "Make yourself at home." Hurrying out, I leave before I can worry any more about this situation I've found myself in.

Before long, I find myself knocking at Scotty's door. Sylvia's surprise is annoying.

"Where's the baby?"

"Uh, Sergey, why are you here?"

"Baby, Sylvia. Where?"

She watches me nervously. "He's upstairs asleep. Lucky for you, the girls are in the backyard."

I brush past her and hurry up the steps. I love her girls, but babies don't talk. That's what I'd like right now. She follows after me. "Serge, I really don't think you should bother him; I just got him down." She huffs when I carefully pick up her sleeping baby. It pisses Sylvia off, but she never stops me either. Mostly because not once have I ever managed to wake the babe up. I take a seat in the rocking chair and she sits in the small recliner.

"What are you doing here, Serge?" she whispers. "Shouldn't you be reuniting with your wife?" Good to know that Scotty came back and told his wife about what happened at my place. "Is everything okay?" When I still don't respond to her, she sighs. "I feel like you're going to steal my baby."

That makes me smile. "I wouldn't," I promise.

"Why do you like him so much?" she asks me curiously.

"Seth doesn't talk back to me; he just listens," I admit. Why not? The world is falling apart. Who cares anymore?

"I can listen."

I laugh quietly, doing my best not to jostle the boy. "You gossip."

"I can keep secrets."

"Can't you leave me alone?"

"I would, but normally, you come over, spend some time with my girls, and then ask to see Seth. Serge, you literally stormed into my house and took my baby out of his crib. I know you well enough by now to know that sometimes, for whatever reason, you spend time with my kids to feel better. Seth may be a good listener, but maybe you need someone to talk to. Do you want me to get Scott?"

I shake my head. Sylvia allows us to sit in silence for a few minutes until she can't take it anymore.

"What happened with you and your wife?" she asks gently.

Most people don't know I even have a wife. I take my privacy to the extreme sometimes. Because of that, it makes discussing my issues even more difficult. But I'm at a loss right now. Holding baby Seth has helped me relax some. It's hard to hold tension in when holding a baby.

"My wife and I were set up by our parents. She hated the idea so much, but couldn't manage to find a way out of it. I liked her, so I didn't mind. But the moment we were married, she skipped out. She wanted nothing to do with me or our marriage. I had hockey to deal with by that point, so we easily went our separate ways. We keep in touch here and there. But now she's here for either a divorce or a baby because our parents are bothering her about that."

Sylvia's eyes widen and she clutches at her chest. "Maybe you two can actually give it a shot."

That makes me smile. I would like that, but I don't see it happening.

"I doubt Galina wants that. Besides, I already told her I would give her the divorce."

"Love always finds a way, Sergey." She stands and pats my shoulder. "Stay as long as you need with Seth, but you are going home to your wife."

CHAPTER 2

GALINA

don't know what I'm doing here. Or if I should stay. My head and heart have been a constant jumble for years. I wouldn't know what was up if there was a neon sign pointing in that direction. My stomach grumbles. One thing I can do right now is cook something for dinner. I don't think Sergey would mind. But maybe I should put away some of my things.

I don't even know if he'll want me to stay, though. Curious nonetheless, I find that Sergey has three empty drawers and space in the closet. Has that space always been empty? Did he reserve that for me in the event I might show up one day? Has he been waiting for me to return all this time? What kind of man does that? Our marriage doesn't even mean anything. Scared to death that I'm yet again making the wrong choice, I hurry and unpack my things before tucking my luggage away in the closet. I'm not sure how long I'm staying, but might as well be comfortable while I'm here.

Then with a little hesitancy, I look through his kitchen to see what I can put together for dinner. Grabbing something here and something there, I slowly begin to put together a meal while feeling thoroughly out of place. As if I'm an intruder. I hate popping into Sergey's life like this, but I need peace. Coming to see him with a set of demands seems like the only way to achieve that. Already the tightness that has been clenching my throat seems to be loosening.

My mind returns to when I told Sergey I'd found comfort from someone else. It was only a fling, but the look on Sergey's face when I told him and to see that he actually wears his ring astonished me. It may just be on a necklace around his neck, but it was more than I expected. My ring has been tucked away in a ring box for years. Sergey looked so betrayed to learn we weren't on the same level with the most basic of things. I can't say I blame him. He can't blame me either, though. Our lives are entirely separate.

He's made quite a nice home for himself. Even though we never truly lived as a married couple or behaved as one, he sent money to me every paycheck. He didn't have to do that, and it felt weird for him to do so. I never spent the money. It's been in a savings account ever since the first check came. I need to make sure I give that back to him.

Now, I'm in his kitchen cooking dinner and our relationship is more of a mess than it was when we were first married. Or even when we first met. Sergey and I hung out together when we were younger. There was palpable chemistry then that led to some kissing and touching here and there. The chemistry smacked me in the face when he opened the door today. It seems to still linger in the air now, though he's not here; I'm trying to ignore it.

However, once my parents told me he was the one I was to marry, it was like everything shut off between us. He was colored in a new light and one I didn't like at all. I couldn't find a way to wiggle out of the wedding, but thankfully, I found excuses not to leave with Sergey when his hockey career took off.

Just as I plate my food, the door to his apartment opens.

He walks back in, seemingly more relaxed. He stops short upon seeing me as if he forgot I was here.

"I hope it's okay; I got hungry."

He nods, but doesn't move or say a word. An awkwardness and uneasiness hangs in the air between us.

"Would you like some?" I ask.

"Okay."

I fix him a plate and then walk around to the other side of the bar and sit down. After a moment, he sits next to me. I almost want to ask him where he went, but I'm not sure I have that privilege. Maybe I don't even want to know.

We eat in silence. No talking. Just the clinking of of silverware against plates. A second after Sergey finishes his meal, he looks at me full of conviction. "Divorce is off the table, Galina. So is a baby." I open my mouth to object, but he raises his hand. "You know I've always cared about you and I know you hate being married to me, but we've never attempted to make it work. Don't you think we should try that first?"

"You mean, actually be married?"

Sergey nods. "You give me three dates to convince you that we stand a chance to make this work. If you think it's hopeless after that, we'll get divorced and I'll handle talking to our parents."

"Okay." What do I have to lose with three little dates? Plus, when it does fall apart completely, I don't have to deal with the aftermath. No one can blame me, because I'm certain our parents will find a way to put this all on me. It's me who is the troublemaker. It's me who won't listen and do what is supposedly my "duty." But if Sergey fights back for me, with me? It's totally different for them. This seems like the perfect out.

He nods, satisfied. "This is good. Thank you. I've missed home cooking; I try to go over to Scotty's every so often so they can feed me something good."

That doesn't surprise me. One of Sergey's favorite things is food, but only if it's made at home. That is something his mother stressed to me in her efforts to make me her son's perfect wife. What a lost cause that was. I finish eating in silence, fatigue wearing me down with every bite. But still, I stand to wash the dishes once I'm finished.

"Galina, leave them."

He doesn't have to convince me, especially when I'm so tired. "I think I want some sleep. I hope it's okay that I unpacked."

Sergey nods. "You are free to make this your home. You can have the bed, too."

With a quick nod, I put some space between us to find something to change into and get ready for bed. A few minutes later, I crawl between his soft sheets. Sergey is putting dishes away, causing me to sigh with relief. Maybe I can fall asleep quickly. The ridiculous nerves of the situation prevent me from falling asleep as fast as I want, though. I lie awake long enough to hear Sergey get ready for bed.

He stands on the other side, curses, and then swipes a pillow. His footsteps move away from the bed and the next rustling I hear sounds as if he's making a bed for himself on the couch.

"Galina?" Sergey whispers after a bit.

"Yeah?"

"This is awkward, yes?"

With a little laugh, I confirm.

"You must have hope this will work out as it should. I know how you like to be a pessimist."

"Okay," I whisper. He's not wrong. I'm not even a glass half empty kind of girl. I'm more of a the glass is broken with water spilling everywhere kind of girl. That's just what my life has turned me into ever since my teenage years.

"Good night."

"Good night, Sergey." I close my eyes, relaxing. Sergey said he'd take me on three dates to convince me we can make this work. I honestly don't know how I feel about that, but it ultimately feels as if it'll be my ticket out of this mess. I keep reminding myself of that. Hope blossoms within for the first time in years at the thought of a resolution, allowing me to fall asleep.

When I awake in the morning, I sit up in time to see Sergey doing the same. The deal we've made is heavy on my mind already.

"Why do you want to do this?" I ask with curiosity. We've been married since we were seventeen, and now we're twenty-six. All these years, we've lived apart. "Why should we try to make it work?" My eyes fall to his bare chest, landing on his wedding band. The sight does funny things to me, things I don't understand.

"People want to know where my wife is when they see it, so I stopped wearing it so I can stop answering that question," he says instead. I can't believe he ever wore it at all, or even long enough that people around him asked questions about it. But then, Sergey did always seem the honorable type. "I know you don't like the decisions our parents made for us, but we ultimately agreed. I wouldn't feel right about divorcing if we didn't at least give it a fair chance."

I nod in agreement about giving it a fair chance, but I'm tempted to argue because I did not agree to this marriage in the first place. No one asked if this was what I wanted. No one cared.

"I have to go work out. We'll talk more when I get back."

I watch him stand and disappear into the bathroom; a few minutes later, he leaves. Sergey is gone longer than I expect and at some point, it's just time to get out of bed to work. I am a full-time instructor at a university. I do very well for myself.

I'm grading assignments when Sergey returns.

"Working?" he asks when he sees me on my computer.

"Yeah."

"How has work been? My mother mentioned you were a teacher for a university now."

"Pretty busy."

He takes a seat next to me. "I'm proud of you," he says.

I smile. "Thank you."

"I should shower." He stands, but then turns to face me. "First date is tomorrow. We're also going to a team party this weekend."

"I have to go?" I was hoping to avoid that for as long as possible, especially after Sergey said no one knows about me. As rightly so as that may be, it will make things awkward.

"Yes." He doesn't give me room to argue; he turns on his heels and stalks to the bathroom like a man on a mission.

Well, that's that, I guess.

CHAPTER 3

SERGEY

Having Galina here is going about like I expected. Things are weird and it's almost as if we're walking on eggshells at times. It feels as if there's an ominous cloud in the room, following us wherever we go. There's more we should discuss, like how this living arrangement will truly work, but we're avoiding it. We're coexisting for the moment.

Today, we go on our date. I'm about as nervous as I was on our very first parent-forced date. I was nervous, but she was extremely annoyed back then.

We're quiet as we get ready, not dressing particularly nice, as we don't need to for this date.

"What kind of place is this?" Galina asks as we arrive at the restaurant.

"We're embracing the Southern cuisine."

She raises her eyebrows at me, but says nothing. There's a reason for this, but I don't want to divulge it yet. My idea seems even more ridiculous than when I first thought of it. Maybe I should grant her the divorce instead of doing this.

"This feels a little like our first date all over again," Galina says with a small laugh after the waitress takes our drink orders.

I nod in agreement.

"Sergey." I glance up, hearing the nervousness in her tone. "There's a man who keeps looking at us with this cheesy grin."

And the jig is up. I look over my shoulder where her gaze rests, but I already know what I'll find. "That's Marco and his wife, Lizzy," I say as I turn to wave at them. "They are our supervision; this is Lizzy's favorite restaurant. They picked it for us." I wait to see if she'll grasp the meaning behind all of that.

Her eyes widen. "This *is* like our first date." She laughs. "Are you going to be polite and try not to like me because you're upset our parents set us up on a date?"

I smile. When our parents arranged for us to go on a date together, I pretended to dislike the idea once I realized Galina wasn't pleased. Her mom sent us to her favorite restaurant, where my parents sat nearby to watch us and make sure we both behaved. "I'll behave."

"How come you chose them and not Scott?" she asks.

"They have twin babies; I figured they could use the night out more than Scott and Sylvia."

Galina nods in understanding. We take some time to look over the menu and I laugh when Galina asks what a hush-puppy is. Eating over at Scotty's, who is originally from the area, means I'm well-versed in the local foods. It might be best if I order for her, so I do with her permission.

"How are your parents?" I ask.

She shrugs. "They stopped talking to me about three years ago because they said I was being stubborn. They couldn't understand why I was still separated from you and they were very frustrated."

My eyes widen. I did not know this. But Galina said she

was still being pressured, which can only mean one thing. "So it is my parents who are hounding you then?"

Galina nods. "But I know my parents are behind it as well."

"I'm sorry. I will talk to them." There's no reason for them to bother her. While they are the reason we are together, we're adults and they need to stay out of our business, what little of it we have.

She waves her hand at my offer. "It's too late for that now. I'm already here. Once we figure out what we're doing, then you can talk to them and get everyone off my back."

The waitress breaks the slight tension by dropping a basket of hushpuppies on the table with our drinks. She gives us an update on how much longer it'll be until our food will be here and then off she goes again. I push the basket toward Galina.

"Try them." We already smelled butter and grease, but now we get the addition of both of those combined with a oniony, bready mix as the hushpuppies join us. "You can dip in the butter too," I tell her as she hesitantly picks one up, examining it.

She decides against the butter. Galina takes a small bite, nods her head, and pops the rest into her mouth.

"I want you to look a new place for us to live."

"Sergey," she starts, and I can hear the protest already.

"The season will start soon and I can't afford to continue sleeping on the couch. Plus, you deserve better." Even if she's here for only a short time, we should still do this. It's not going to matter to me if I upgrade my living arrangements and it's still just me; it'll be worth it for something that better suits Galina for the time being and so I won't have to resort to sleeping on my couch.

Galina stares at me for a moment. "We're adults. We can share until we figure out what we're doing; or I can sleep on the couch."

I don't like that idea. However, there's only so much one can push Galina; I'll accept this for now. "How much are you dreading the party this weekend?"

Galina groans, which makes me laugh. "More than you can imagine. Most people don't even know you have a wife and now you're showing up with someone who isn't really your wife. It sounds like there will be so much focus on us."

"The good news is that the person who would annoy us the most already knows. But if we're going to do this, then it's time we do things together." Even if we won't be together for long.

"Why?" she asks. "Your mom says you hate team parties and unless it was stressed you had to be there, you didn't go."

True. I wasn't much of a teammate before compared to the way things are run here, but things are different now. "I like this team." I may not be expressive about it, but I do like them. "They invite me, I go."

Galina sighs. "What is the party for?"

"It's just a party. Anyone who is in town was invited. Something to get everyone together. Let the kids have some fun." I shrug. "Someone was bored and wanted to throw a party." As far as I can tell, there's no actual reason for us to get together.

"What have you been doing with your time?" she asks about halfway through our meal.

I relax with her question. "Hockey. Getting teammates to feed me. I hang out at Scotty's a lot and spend time with his kids. He has two twin girls and a baby boy. I teach the girls Russian and about Russia. Since the baby can't talk, I tell him things."

Galina opens her mouth, but she doesn't get a chance to speak before Marco and Lizzy walk up to our table.

"Supervision time is over; Elizabeth is anxious to get home to the babies." He looks at Galina. "Did he tell you I delivered them?" I swear his chest puffs out.

Lizzy laughs and shakes her head. "No one cares but you, Marc. Thanks for helping us get a little break, Serge. We'll see you this weekend, right?"

"Yes. Thank you."

They say their goodbyes and Lizzy drags Marco away before he can get distracted by talking some more. Galina looks at me once they've walked away. "You like kids?" she asks with a puzzled look.

"Yes. At some point, I'd want one of my own. Don't you?"

She nods. "But I've wasted a lot of time. Part of me feels too old."

I laugh. "You are not old, Galina."

She shrugs her shoulders and that seems to be that. Food has slowly disappeared from both of our plates. The waitress stops by to take my card and this nagging question, which has no right, simply refuses to leave my mind.

"Can I ask you something?" I finally ask.

Again, she shrugs as she takes another long pull on her straw.

"How long was the affair?"

Galina chokes slightly. She sputters before clearing her throat, looking at me with wild eyes. "*Affair*?" A string of fast, nasty Russian curses spews from her mouth to assault my ears as she stands. The scraping of her chair as she stands is loud, even in the busy restaurant. "You bastard!" she breathes, her chest heaving. "Accusing me of such a thing." Galina flings her napkin on the table with a flair of dramatics. "Go to hell."

"Galina!" I shout as she storms toward the exit. Just as I scan the room for the waitress, I find her hurrying my way with my card. I snatch it, mutter a thanks, and run after Galina. Where she thinks she's going, I'm not sure. She's trying to cross the street it seems. Running faster, I try to catch her. Affair wasn't the best choice of words, but it was the only one coursing through my mind.

The sound of a rumbling engine hits me first. And then I see the car from the corner of my eye. Galina doesn't appear to be paying attention, wrapped up so much in her anger.

"Galina!" I shout again. I push my legs harder. Relief fills me as I reach out to wrap my fingers around her wrist and then yank her back to me. The car speeds past us as if we're not even standing here and as if they didn't almost run her over. "You okay?" I ask, turning her to face me.

"I'm fine!" she snaps, wiggling out of my hold. "Are you telling me you haven't been with anyone else, Sergey? Truly? No one? No one at all? Not even once?"

My hands fall to my sides. I slowly shake my head. Her eyes widen as it sinks in. "But we were only seventeen. Are you... Does that mean you're a..."

I laugh, realizing what she's asking. "I haven't been with anyone since we got married." My smile falls away. "Whether you were here or not, temptations or not, I couldn't break those vows." There have been many times I've thought about it. Many, many times. Nine years is a long time. I've been on the precipice of breaking those vows, but then it's like a stone wall falls down before me as quickly as the urge came to be. Reality hits and it's as if the woman's face morphs into Galina's. I simply can't do it, knowing it isn't actually her in front of me. Many times, it has felt like a curse.

Galina takes another step back with her disbelief. She stumbles as her foot slips off the curb. Like a snake striking its prey, my hand reaches out and I pull her back to me. She steadies, but only because she's leaning against me. Galina stares at me for a moment. Her eyes narrow, crinkling at the corners.

"How do I know you aren't lying?"

Something within me snaps. Perhaps it's the nine years of abstinence. Nine years of waiting around on a woman who never wanted to come around anyway. Nine years of doing what was *right*. And she has the gall to question me? Question my faithfulness? Question my honesty?

Who the fuck does she think she is?

I drop my hold, step backward, and she nearly falls as she was still on the edge of the curb.

"Find your own way home." Turning on my heels, I storm off to my SUV. I have done nothing to cause her to doubt me. Never have I lied to her. I haven't been given many opportunities, but still. Fury bubbles within me that she would question me. Leaving Galina at the restaurant feels wrong and irresponsible, but she's a big girl.

In actuality, I make it half a mile before turning around. I park nearby to spy on Galina. She's standing close to the curb still, waiting. Anger over her insinuating I was lying pulses through my veins enough that I don't go get her. Instead, I wait and watch. A few minutes pass and a car pulls up. She gets in and I follow behind. Pissed off or not, I can still make sure she finds her way back safely.

If this is how date one went, I have no idea how we're going to make it through two more. Maybe she was right all along and we should get a divorce.

CHAPTER 4

GALINA

"This is good news, yes? You are living with Sergey, so now your marriage can continue. You two can reconnect and finally have children."

Why did I answer the phone call from his mother? It's hard not to, honestly. Partly out of respect to them and partly because it's not like I would be ignoring my own parents. I'm ignoring someone else's parents and that seems to take the level of wrongness to, well, another level. Or maybe I'm a glutton for punishment.

"Actually, we're contemplating divorce."

The gasp she makes is so loud and startled that I feel horrible. I'm probably about to give the poor woman a heart attack.

"You can't do that! You two were meant for one another!"

Are we, though? Would it really be the worst thing in the world if Sergey and I *finally* went our separate ways to forge our own paths in life? I don't think it would. Hell, I've been trying to do that for years already, but you can't really move forward when something like this is following you around ever so closely.

"Mrs. Orlovsky, please," I say just as Sergey walks in the

door. His entire expression hardens at immediately realizing I'm on the phone with his mother. He storms over to where I sit at the bar, plucks the phone from my hand, and shocks me as much as I just shocked his mother. In our native language, he berates his mother so fluently and strongly that it overwhelms me.

And turns me on?

I shake my head to shoo those thoughts away. Sure, he said he would handle his parents, mine too if needed, but I never thought he actually would. All these years, no one has bothered standing up for me when I needed help. Why would now be any different?

Yet, here Sergey is. Talking to his mother as if she's a child in need of a stern talking-to. I most definitely swoon.

Sergey paces as he speaks. His mother barely gets a word in edgewise, but within a few minutes, he tells her he loves her and hangs up. He hands my phone back to me with one hand while the other runs through his hair.

"She won't be bothering you again," he reassures me.

My eyes widen. I was so lost in watching him that I didn't even pay attention to the actual conversation. She really won't call again? Is he sure?

"I'm sorry you've been dealing with that. They don't even mention you when they call me."

I huff. Of course they don't. Why bother Sergey with what they think needs to be done? It's all supposed to be up to me. I'm the problem anyway. "Thank you," I finally tell him, truly grateful.

He nods. After a moment, he says, "You told her we were divorcing?"

"That we're thinking of it." I shrug. "I don't know what I was hoping to accomplish with that." With a sigh, I hide my face in my hands. The weight of both of our parents' expectations has overwhelmed me for so long. I've tried to ignore it and move on, but being here with Sergey and knowing that soon, one way or another, this fiasco will be dealt with has brought it all back to the forefront. Exhaustion weighs me down to the point I feel as if I'm drowning.

Sergey closes the distance between us and envelops me in his arms. "You should have told me sooner."

"I don't need someone else telling me what I should have done or should be doing," I snap into his chest. Does he not see I've been doing the best I can?

"I'm just saying I was never supposed to be your enemy."

My shoulders sag. "I know." He was an enemy by association. I'm still not sure where he stands on that ground either. He left me to find my own way home from the disaster of our first date. It's been a few days since then and we've been walking on eggshells around one another.

What has startled me, though, is this side of Sergey that I've never seen before. I didn't know these things exist in men. Even my own father doesn't do what I've witnessed from Sergey this week. He's cooked a meal or two, but even if I cook, he always washes the dishes afterward. He's asked if I needed any clothes washed when he did laundry. He's gone grocery shopping and has even picked up some snacks for me, without even asking. I can only imagine that he knows what I like from the little time we voluntarily spent time together all those years ago or from my mother, way back when they started pushing us together.

He's sweet. Certainly doesn't seem like he expects anything out of me. It seems as if he truly sees me as an equal, as a partner in this mess. It's changed my view of him and in a good way. Being here to see his movements, his body...it's messing with my mind. Or, more accurately, other parts of my body. For so long, I've directed my anger with my parents, with this situation, at Sergey too and it's slowly dawning on me, with each peek of that ring hanging from his neck, that I've been a fool to do so.

He's right. He's an ally and I should have at least considered him one.

"The party is today."

"I know," I groan. Sergey chuckles as I sit up to look at him, causing his arms to fall back by his sides. "You aren't going to leave me there, are you?"

"You aren't going to get pissed and nearly get yourself run over by a car and then call me a liar, are you?" he asks with narrowed eyes.

Deciding now isn't the time to dive into it, I shrug. "We'll have to see." Swiveling away from him and his too-intense gaze, I mutter, "I have to get ready."

I'm dreading this party so much. Why does Sergey have to do this to me? It spells disaster. How will he introduce me? Are they really nice people? Even if so, will they be nice to me? Why invite me when they'll ask questions when I undoubtedly disappear soon? Just because Sergey stood up to his mother for me doesn't mean I think this thing between us will actually work. Yet, he's integrating me into his life as if it will. My stomach launches to my throat as I get ready and then as Sergey drives us over to his teammate's house.

The party is hopping in the backyard when we arrive. Sergey leads me that way with a hand on my lower back. I don't know whether to stick to his side or run far, far away.

At first, no one notices us.

And then...

"Sergey!"

The little girl who shouted his name runs full speed toward him. His hand falls away from me and he crouches to catch her as she barrels into him. Within seconds, a second girl follows. He rocks on his heels from the impact.

"Hello, Stephanie. And I can't forget you, too, Stella. How are you two today?" he asks.

"We've been waiting for you!" they say together.

And then one of them notices me. I'm not sure which.

"Who are you?"

"This is Galina. I'll need you two to help me keep an eye on her and make sure she has fun, okay?"

The girls eye me with a little suspicion, but nod. One little girl takes my hand while the other takes Sergey's.

"Come with us. Momma said to bring you over when you got here."

Sergey chuckles but allows them to drag us. And that's when I realize everyone is trying their hardest not to gawk at us. I told Sergey this would be awkward. How can he just show up with a woman? And if he introduces me as his wife? Even worse, especially if things fall through.

I really want to go home.

"Can you speak Russian too?" the little girl asks me as we walk.

I nod, but then I realize she's asked me in Russian. I smile and respond in kind. She smiles brightly.

"My name is Stella," she tells me, and then in English, "Sergey has been teaching us, but Momma got us classes too. Sergey is more fun."

I laugh. "You are learning very well."

"Thank you!" she beams.

The girls have finished their job of leading us over to a picnic table where a group of people have gathered. One of them I recognize as the man who was in Sergey's apartment the day I arrived, who turns out to be the girls' father.

"Okay, who is she?"

I blink at the person who asks upon realizing he's sitting next to someone who looks exactly like him. How many twins are walking around this place? The brother slaps the speaker in the back of the head.

"Don't be rude, Cal."

"We're all wanting to know," he says.

"Her name is Galina. That is who she is," Sergey states

with a note of finality. I wait for more questions, but not a soul asks a follow-up question.

Well, he's not saying I'm his wife, so that's good.

I'm quickly introduced to entirely too many people. Sergey then leaves me with someone named Sylvia, claiming I'm in good hands, while he supposedly runs off to grab us something to drink. Sylvia nestles a baby to her chest. She tells me his name is Seth. I nod. Everyone seems to be watching me, still. Meanwhile, I spot Sergey, off chatting away with someone.

He actually looks happy and in his element.

"You look like a fish out of water."

"I'm sorry?" I bring my attention back to my party caretaker.

"You look very uncomfortable," Sylvia repeats. She leans in closer. "I know who you actually are." If possible, I stop breathing. "I'm quite fond of your husband. Almost more than anyone else on the team aside from my own husband. He's a good man and why the hell you don't want him quite frankly makes me wonder what the hell is wrong with *you*. If you don't see it, then Sergey needs to ignore my advice to give it a go and run as far away as he can."

She leaves me stunned as she leans away as if she wasn't even talking to me. Upon her dismissal, it seems as if everyone else takes her cue and realizes I'm nothing worth paying attention to after all.

This is almost as bad as being back home. Anytime I've decided to venture back home, it's as if my family does a one-eighty. As if their disappointment is so great, it's too much to interact with me. I'm largely ignored, possibly as punishment for my actions. Even here, the same thing is happening. Can I not go anywhere without my marriage and those who support it making me feel so minuscule?

I stand up to go find myself something to drink. Or, that's what I'm telling myself is the reason I'm getting up. This is too hard; I wish I never came to find Sergey. The reward was not worth it. There is no reward. There rarely is in my life.

I spot a cooler on the other side of the pool and head that way. A few people are in the pool. Someone is manning a grill. Seems like quite a few people are in town, but then I don't know how many people normally show up for these parties.

As I walk by the pool, kids run toward me. They are chasing each other and it looks like Stella might have a tight squeeze between me and a chair that wasn't pushed in. I turn sideways to give her more room, but Stella bumps into me just as I turn. It's enough that I lose my balance and fall backward into the pool with a small shriek.

Luckily, no one is behind me. I surface with a sputter to see a group of horrified little kids staring at me.

"It's fine," I immediately tell them. No one pushed me intentionally, and the last thing I want is to be the reason these kids get in trouble. "I was planning to go for a swim anyway."

"In your clothes?" Stella asks, not buying my story.

"Yep."

"Galina!" Sergey skids to a stop next to the kids, looking equally horrified.

"I'm fine," I repeat. "Decided to go for a dip."

Parents start shouting kids' names and one by one, they disperse.

"Are you going to get out?" he asks.

I shake my head. While a complete accident, I'm embarrassed. Enough attention has been drawn to me and if I can hide in the pool for a bit, that sounds like a great idea.

He kicks off his shoes and socks, sits on the edge, even though his ass is totally getting soaked from the splash I just made, and wiggles his finger for me to come over. "Why won't you get out?"

"Because being in this pool relatively alone is the best part of this party," I admit.

Sergey frowns. He shocks the hell out of me by then sliding into the pool. Neither of us have a change of clothes, so this is perfect. Grabbing my hips, he pulls me close.

Quietly and in Russian, he talks to me. "Let me guess. Sylvia said something probably not nice, but something that was looking out for me. People are giving you entirely too much space and not talking to you. That's probably my fault since I'm not overly talkative. And lastly, you feel out of place here."

"She's that predictable?" I can't help but ask.

Sergey laughs. It's kind of nice to see him laugh. He's relaxed around these people. "Yes. Do you want me to tell her off? She won't listen, but I can do it."

I shake my head.

"I'm so sorry!" We look up to see Sylvia, who has come to apologize on behalf of her daughter. "Stella told me what happened."

A couple walks up. "How can I help?" the woman asks. The man just chuckles while looking at Sergey.

"We're okay, Julie," Sergey says. "Stop laughing, Collin. She's fine," he adds. "We're going to head home to change."

I guess that means we're coming back? Great.

Sergey lifts himself out of the pool and then turns to hold a hand out for me. He pulls me out and Julie offers us towels before scurrying inside to get us some. I tune out while Sergey and Sylvia smooth the incident over with one another. Julie quickly returns with a set of towels, handing them both to Sergey. He wraps one around my shoulders. I shiver as he runs his hands up and down my arms for a few seconds. He then wraps a towel around himself.

Finally, he excuses us and we're on our way.

"Are you sure you're not upset?" he asks once we're in the car.

"Yes. I'm okay."

We ride in silence until we return to his apartment. Sergey takes my hand before I can step too far away from him.

"Galina." I turn to face him, wondering why he's seemingly more attractive right now. His hair is a little wacky. Strands moving all kinds of ways. His shirt hugs his skin. Physical attraction means nothing. I've been attracted to plenty of people over the years; nothing ever come of that either. "Galina?"

I snap out of my ogling. "Yes?"

He grins. "I asked you a question."

"What was it?"

Instead of answering, he asks, "What are you thinking? What were you looking at?"

I narrow my eyes. "What was your actual question?"

"Are you finding me attractive right now, Galina?" The teasing in his tone is slightly annoying.

"Why would I do that?"

He takes a step closer to me. "Because I'm naturally handsome."

I can't help but laugh. I didn't expect that kind of response from him. He runs his hands up my arms, causing an involuntary shiver. "We should change. You told them we would go back." And this suddenly feels like a dangerous situation. He stands entirely too close and looks entirely too attractive. Which, he's always been attractive, but we never crossed that line, even after we married. Yes, that's right. I've never had sex with my husband. Our parents fully expected us to, but Sergey didn't pressure me or even mention it once. I took full advantage of that.

"Galina." His voice is low and sultry. Why does he keep saying my name? Why is it so hot? He tilts his head down just a little. My breathing shallows. He's so close. "If I kissed you, would you let me? Or would you slap me?"

Is he asking for permission? I can't even believe he's mentioning it. Is this something I actually want to do?

Before I can contemplate it any longer, he kisses me. He actually kisses me! His lips press to mine. At first, softly. Tentatively. Then harder with more conviction. And it's...it's heavenly. My body comes alive as if it's been dormant all this time. My hands turn into fists, clutching his shirt. My back slams against a wall, but what distracts me is that Sergey's body then presses against mine.

I nearly moan when I feel his hands slip underneath my shirt.

"Should we stop?" he mumbles as his lips skitter across my neck.

This feels like a fork in the road moment. My heart pounds against my chest. Thump, thump, thumping as hard as it can. While my mind debates, I hear myself breathe, "No."

CHAPTER 5

SERGEY

Galina's head rests on my shoulder. Her leg is thrown over my hips and her fingers have tangled themselves with my necklace, my wedding band nestled in her grasp. She fell asleep pretty soon after our tangle in the sheets. I'm not sure if that's a good sign or not. Either she was so satisfied she passed out or she has a sudden feeling of regret and she decided sleep was the best route. Her body betrayed her while she slept, though.

This seems like a good sign, but with Galina, who knows. She stirs slightly, enough that I think she's awake now. I have no idea what to say, so I remain silent.

"Will they be upset that we didn't go back to the party?" she asks after what seems like forever.

"That's what you're thinking about right now?" I can't help but chuckle. Of all the things I thought she would say, that wasn't one of them.

Galina shrugs. "I feel like we're living in a bubble this very second and it'll burst soon." She pauses and quietly adds, "I don't think I want it to."

"Now you like me?" I tease.

"I like you enough," she agrees. She's quiet for a moment before she adds, "That was never the issue." That I already knew. Galina sighs. "Part of me thinks if we do manage to make it work, it will be worse than if we divorce. My parents will likely swoop back in and overwhelm me, demanding a baby again. I just want peace. Why is that too much to ask?"

She sounds exhausted and sad. It's as if no matter which path she takes, she's expecting negative results. As if her life is doomed and she loses either way.

The words coming out of my mouth go against every fiber of my being, but so be it. "Stop talking to them. Our parents. Ignore them, tell me, and I'll be the go-between. No matter what happens, I will always be your ally. Let me deal with those battles."

"Maybe that will work." She doesn't sound like she has any faith that it will, but that isn't surprising for how negative her outlook can be. I'll take it.

Something has been weighing on my mind since earlier today, and hoping she'll tell me, I ask, "What did Sylvia say to you?"

Without any hesitation, she says, "She told me she knew who I was and that you were a good man. She basically thinks something is wrong with me because I didn't want to be with you, and that if I can't see what's right in front of me, then you should run far away from me."

That's a bit harsh. Sylvia doesn't know enough about Galina or our background to be so forthcoming with her thoughts.

Galina surprises the hell out of me by continuing with, "She's right, though." Her fingers finally release from my necklace. "I'm not saying I'm in love with you or anything, but," she props herself up on her elbow, "I've been so angry with our parents and I lumped you in with them when I shouldn't have. We enjoyed ourselves when we spent time together before, but..." She shakes her head, seemingly at a loss for words.

"It was tainted by us getting married," I finish.

She nods, a sad smile on her face. For the first time in years, I actually feel hopeful. This is the most progress we've ever made and it's something. It doesn't have to be all or nothing with us, I realize. Right now, all or *something* works. She's giving me something. We can work on the all part later.

"We can stay in our bubble for as long as you'd like," I tell her.

The smile Galina gives me rocks the very core of my being. The warmth of her body pressed against me with all of the hills and valleys is suddenly impossible to ignore. Taking a chance, I grab her thigh and pull her on top of me. Her eyebrow lifts.

"Our bubble requires years of catching up, physically and otherwise."

Her lips twitch with a smile. "Whatever you say, Sergey."

———

I promised Galina three dates. I still owe her two, but I'm struggling to think of what to do with them. Ideas will come to me, I'm sure. Since the team party, things have been better with us. The only tension that remains is sexual tension. The downside is that since I last spoke to my mother, advising her to leave Galina alone, I'm getting more phone calls. A taste of what Galina had to deal with is what I now get to experience. In an odd way, I'm thankful. It's easier to see things from her point of view.

It's tiring to have to speak to them so often and about my relationship with Galina. So far, I've been limiting the information to nothing of substance. I've been hinting that it's none of their business in hopes that they'll stop asking, but no such luck so far.

Today, though, I somehow got roped into taking Scotty's girls, Stephanie and Stella, and Raelynn's son, Jackson, to the local ice rink. Possibly even more surprising is that Galina decided to come along. The kids just wanted some ice time to skate. The twins are a bit competitive with one another and Jackson has been learning.

"Will you skate with us too?" Stephanie asks me after they've laced up.

I wouldn't mind, but there's Galina.

When I glance at her, she smirks. "I know how to skate too."

Ah, that's right. She dabbled in figure skating when she was younger. With that, I confirm that I will be on the ice with the kids. Galina heads over to the rental counter for a pair of skates while the rest of us lace up our personal skates. The kids hit the ice as soon as they are ready, but I hang back, waiting for Galina.

It's crazy how practically any ice rink can feel like a second home of sorts. My muscles relax the moment I see the gleam of the ice. My lungs breathe a little easier. Galina likely doesn't feel quite the same. I believe her skating was pushed on her by her parents.

The kids request my presence to participate in races, so I happily oblige. Galina keeps to herself, skating as if she's been doing so regularly all these years. After a bit, the kids seem content to entertain theirselves and I skate over to Galina.

"It's weird seeing you with kids."

I glance over at her, curious. "In a good way or bad?"

"Good. It's just something I didn't really connect with you, but then, I still see seventeen-year-old Sergey most of the times." She surprises me by reaching over and taking my hand. A flicker of a smile plays on her lips. "It's startling to see that in my head and then look at you. Very different."

"How so?" I ask.

"You're definitely not a teenager anymore." Her eyes give me a quick once-over.

I laugh. "Neither are you." Pulling her snug against me, I kiss her quickly, mindful of the kids with us today. Being physical with her seems easy and natural. The rest? We're still working on that aspect. "I'll round the kids up and we'll get ice cream before we take them home."

"Sounds good."

After getting ice cream and dropping the kids off, we return home. An idea has formed about our next date by that time. I'll have to look into that later.

"Why did my mom ask for a grandchild if we weren't together?" I ask, curious. After spending time with the kids today, children in general are on my mind and I'm trying to figure why my mother would push that on her. What's the logic behind it?

Galina shrugs with a sigh. "I don't know. She tried to tell me I was getting up in age and that now was the time to act if I ever wanted children. She said that I was holding you back from having kids by not being with you, and keeping her from grandchildren because I was neglecting our marriage. That's the gist of it." She cocks her head at me, tucking her legs underneath her on the couch as I take a seat next to her. "She really never mentioned us to you?"

"No. She never even asked if we spoke or what my plans were in regard to the marriage."

She rolls her eyes and looks irritated. That's not really the mood I want her to be in and I regret asking. On the other hand, I'm glad to know more about what she dealt with specifically with my parents. It also causes my anger to rise at my parents. They have no business talking to Galina like that.

"I'm sorry." I feel like I've apologized a lot on their behalf lately.

Galina smiles. "It's not your fault."

The rest of the afternoon, I pepper her about the time we've spent apart, to learn more about her. We discuss what we currently see and want for our future. When she steps away to shower, I take time to plan our next date.

CHAPTER 6

GALINA

For the first time in years, I receive a call from my mom. It startles me so much and causes my lungs to seize in panic so that all I can do is stare at the screen until it goes to voicemail.

The last time we spoke is so clear in my mind. She asked me if I had any intentions of ever having a life with Sergey. When I answered no, she lost her mind. She went on and on about what it took to apparently convince his parents to agree to the union, how much money went into the wedding, and that I was ruining lives. She told me she was officially done with me and I was no longer her daughter.

A few months after that is when the calls from Sergey's mom started.

"Galina?"

I snap out of the memory and look over at Sergey. He's taking me out for our next date.

"What's wrong?"

"My mom just called. I don't know what to do."

"Do you want to talk to her?" he asks.

Do I? She's my mother and I love her dearly, despite our issues. But those issues have caused an enormous strain on our relationship. Obviously, since we no longer talk. I wonder if she's only calling now because Sergey's mom told her I'm here with him. Does she plan to start pressuring me again?

Sensing my hesitation and uncertainty, Sergey reaches over to hold my hand. Comfort seems to emit from his body straight into mine. "Remember, I'm your ally. You don't want to talk to her, don't. You want me to talk to her, I will. You are not in this alone anymore."

That's such an unfamiliar feeling. No one has ever had my back before and it definitely makes me swoon every time Sergey talks about how he has mine.

"Let's not think about it for now." With that decision, I toss my phone into one of the cupholders of his car and decide that I don't need it for the time being. "What are we doing anyway?" My question comes too late almost because he pulls into a parking lot.

"I remembered that you love ballet and there's a performance here tonight."

For the second time today, I'm stunned. Not only that he remembered, but that he's choosing to take me here for a date. This doesn't seem like his kind of outing at all.

Sergey laughs as he sees my expression. "You don't think I can endure a ballet performance for you?"

"I wouldn't have thought you'd want to," I confirm.

"I don't, but what's a couple hours of boredom if it makes you happy?"

He seems utterly unfazed by it all. As crazy as it sounds, no one has ever endured anything, big or small, for me and my own enjoyment. It gives me the warm and fuzzies that Sergey is doing this.

"Ready?" Sergey asks, hesitating due to my silence.

"Yes."

About thirty minutes into the performance, a low snoring sound emits from Sergey. I smile at seeing his head tilted forward a little, his eyes closed, and his breathing steady. I guess he wasn't lying about being bored. I contemplate waking him, but he's not disturbing anyone. Should he be awake and alert for our date? It's more humorous than anything to me.

I decide to let him be. Three-fourths of the way through the show, Sergey suddenly startles himself awake. He glances over at me, likely to see if I noticed, but I keep my focus on the stage. While he may not have enjoyed himself, I have.

At the end, as we are walking back to his vehicle, I can't help but tease him. "What did you think of the show?"

A flicker of panic crosses his face. "It was good."

"Did you like the solo performance done after the first intermission?"

His eyes widen a little more and it takes some restraint not to laugh. The performance I'm asking about doesn't exist, so his answer will be interesting.

"Yes, very good."

I can't help but laugh and he gives me a curious glance as he opens the door for me.

"I wish I had seen it then." When his brows furrow in confusion, I add, "There wasn't a solo; I'm just teasing since you were sleeping."

For a brief moment, he has a deer in the headlights look. "I was not. I was checking my eyelids for holes."

His answer catches me off guard and I can't help but release a full belly laugh.

"Didn't find any," he adds, nudging me into the car.

"Heading home now?" I ask, still laughing a little as he pulls out of the parking lot.

"Dinner first."

While he drives us to the restaurant, I check my phone to see an additional call from my mother and one from Sergey's. I don't really know what to do with this. My phone is plucked out of my hands and dropped back into the cupholder. I expect Sergey to say something, but he remains silent, and I decide I don't really want to say anything either.

Once we're settled in at the very nice restaurant, he makes conversation with me.

"Do you always teach in the summer?"

"No. Only if there's a need. My fall courses will be starting soon," I explain.

"Will you have to leave?" he asks.

I smile. "No; I got lucky and everything is remote for me."

He learns more about my work, what I teach, and the like. Conversation seems to flow much easier than on our first date. Maybe this could work. Or maybe it never will with our parents looming over me and pushing their wants into me. It's too much to deal with and I don't have the strength to do it. Nor do I have the courage to cut them off completely.

Which makes me think of us. Whatever that exactly entails.

"What are you hoping to get out of this?" I ask him, motioning between the two of us later as he drives us home.

"You staying is all. I hope you'll see there's something between us and you'll stay for us to figure it out. I'm not exactly hoping to get..." He pauses and laughs. "I was going to say married, but that's not quite right. We're married, but we're not a couple. If you stay, maybe we can continue seeing what happens. Maybe we'll stay together; maybe we'll get a divorce." He shrugs. "But at least we'll have tried and done so on our own terms."

That I can deal with and handle. If he was hoping for me to put my wedding ring on at the end of three dates, then I'd have to go ahead and let him down. Not happening. Just because I'm good with potentially sticking around and dating him, doesn't mean I think we're prepared to embrace married life.

"If you decide you want to stay with me, that's fine,"

Sergey continues. "If you want your own space, I'll help you find something."

Us living together brings something else to mind. Something where the topic may piss Sergey off, and I don't want to ruin a good afternoon and evening by making him angry. At the same time, I can't help myself.

"There's something I think we still need to discuss."

A worried glance comes my way.

"The money you send."

Sergey interrupts me with a no-nonsense tone. "You're still my wife, Galina. Please just let me do that; donate it, keep it, invest it, I don't care."

"So far, I've just saved it. I was actually hoping to give it back to you." I peek over at him to see his jaw clenched.

"This has t0 be the least of our issues." A hard exhale pushes through his nose. "If it'll make you feel better, okay, but I'd rather you donate it if you don't want to keep it."

It's not much, but it's a compromise. I'll take it.

Since he's taken to holding my hand while he drives, I give his a squeeze of appreciation.

When he parks, he says, "Our last date, you pick. I'll go and do whatever you want me to do."

"Anything I want?" This is surprising to me. I've always thought of Sergey as being one who'd rather be in charge and make the decisions.

"Anything," he confirms.

This could get very interesting; I'll have to think long and hard about what will be the best and most fun date.

CHAPTER 7

SERGEY

"How are things with your wife?" Scotty asks one night when I come over for dinner. They invited Galina to come, and I relayed that, but she decided to stay behind. I'm perfectly okay with that. She doesn't have to go with me everywhere, especially at this stage in our relationship. She is still a wife who isn't quite my wife.

"We're making progress. Things are good. I think she may stay."

"That's great," he says.

"If she doesn't, I can always play matchmaker," Sylvia offers. "I've been successful in the past."

Scott cuts a look at her, but I just chuckle. She means well. I think she's slightly upset that Galina stayed behind. She's unable to chat with her, learn more about her, and be nosy. I'm sure Galina isn't missing out.

While things have been going well with us, I feel like Galina still has some reservations. That's fine. There's a long history, even if some of it is devoid of any interactions; I can't expect too much. That would be unfair. She's had to deal with way more regarding our so-called relationship than I have.

"She's not still upset over the pool incident, is she?" Sylvia asks. She's been trying to figure out why Galina decided to stay home.

"No. Next time, she'll come," I promise.

"Not everyone is a social butterfly," Scott tells her with a teasing tone.

Still, she frowns. Scott changes the subject to the upcoming season. It will be interesting to see what it will be like, coming and going from home with Galina nearby. I'm not sure if she'll want to live together or if she'll want to get her own space. Our biggest obstacle, still, I believe is our parents.

Galina seems to like me well enough that we likely could have a good thing going if they would simply butt out. Her demeanor has already changed since she's been here. Not a lot, but some. She has stopped talking to either of our parents, though, and I think that's helped with her stress levels.

It actually pisses me off. I also feel like an idiot for not knowing any of this was happening. We could have resolved our issues much sooner if I'd know Galina was being harassed by our parents. Part of me blames her for not reaching out, but I also blame myself for not asking.

The season is fast approaching and I'm really hoping this is somewhat settled by then. It'll be really interesting to see what it'll be like to have a companion around when playing. I haven't ever really had that before. It'll be nice. At least if this doesn't work and we do divorce, I can finally move on and find someone. Or maybe I'll sow my wild oats, though it's a bit late in my life to be doing so.

Galina paces about the apartment when I return.

"I don't think this will ever work," she says the moment she sees me. "We're always going to have our parents to deal with; they will always be hovering in the background and looming over us. I'll always be under their thumb. If I succumb to this, what else will they pressure me to do?"

I grab her hands from her hips and give them a little squeeze. If I had to guess, she got a call from one of our parents and decided to answer. "Galina," I begin softly. "Remember, I'll take care of that; you don't have to."

"But will it be enough? They already know they can force me to marry."

My brows furrow at her comment; she's said it before, but I don't understand it. "Galina, we agreed back then and we've agreed to try now."

Her brows match mine and her voice rises in anger. "Agreed? Why do you keep saying that? I didn't agree to anything! No one asked me what I wanted, Sergey. How exactly did I agree if I was told what I was going to do?"

I frown. "I don't understand."

"That's makes two of us," she cuts in.

"Your parents didn't ask if you'd be willing to marry me and agree to the match?"

"No!" she shrieks incredulously. Her eyes widen, turning wild and livid. "You *were* asked? You *consented*? Why? Why would you do that? I can't believe they wanted your approval, but not mine." She yanks her hands out of mine and paces again, throwing her hands around while she rants. "But of *course* they would want Mr. Perfect, Mr. Success to agree. Who gives a flying fuck what *I* want." She whirls to face me. "I can't believe you agreed." The anger leaves her tone and she's just defeated.

"I thought you did," I reply quietly with a shrug of my shoulders. "We were friends, Galina, and I liked you. I figured it couldn't hurt to say yes and see what happens."

She shakes her head in disbelief as if she's trying to shake off the news. "I need some space." She runs out of the apartment.

I think about calling after her, wishing to comfort her, but the disappointment in her gaze haunts me. Guilt bubbles up inside me as I collapse onto my couch. Should I even feel guilty? Sure, I'm part of why she's in this mess, but I didn't know we weren't treated equally. I genuinely thought we both entered this, knowing it was what our parents wanted, but we were still okay with moving forward.

Maybe I should give her the divorce. She is likely better off with a fresh start than the mess we're currently in. I still like her, though. In all likelihood, if not for our parents, we would've never been together anyway, despite being friends. I would've left town and who knows what Galina would have done. We probably wouldn't have kept in touch. We would have gone our separate ways and never looked back. Maybe that's what we need to do now.

Thinking of potentially telling our parents this makes my stomach hurt. I can only imagine what it's been like for Galina if I feel like this after only a short time of dealing with them. Maybe we'll both cut them out of our lives.

Right now, though, my primary focus is Galina. She wants space, she can have it all. I'll be fine if she walks away, though I truly don't want her to. Galina hasn't had a fair shake once. Maybe I need to stop being selfish, hoping something comes of a relationship with her, and let her go. For once in her life, someone needs to think of her. Perhaps a divorce would be best.

CHAPTER 8

GALINA

I shouldn't be surprised. I shouldn't be upset. This is just run of the mill for me.

But I am surprised and I am upset. With my parents, with his parents, and even with Sergey. He seemed genuine when he said he didn't know, but still. Why agree at all? The pressure and turmoil I've had to endure is partly due to his decision. How can I not blame him?

I drive around for an hour, eventually having to use the GPS to direct me back home since I end up being utterly lost. While I don't feel any better, it feels like it's time.

Sergey sits up straight from his spot on the couch when I walk in. His mouth opens, but I hold my hand to stop him from speaking. Emotionally and mentally, I'm drained. It's as if all the energy has been sucked from my body and there's no way for me to recharge.

After freshening up in the bathroom and changing into pajamas, I crawl into bed and close my eyes. All I want is sleep. Good, long, deep sleep. A few moments later, I hear Sergey moving around and then the light turns off. The bed creaks as he crawls beneath the covers on the other side.

Why does my life have to be so difficult? Why is it so hard for me to have some control over my life? Is that really too much to ask for?

"I'm so sorry, Galina," Sergey whispers, apparently unable to remain silent. He pulls me into his arms, kisses my shoulder, and repeats his apology. When he begins to pull away, I grab his arm.

What's wrong with me? Even upset, I find comfort from Sergey. My emotions are all over the place. I'll figure out what to do with them tomorrow. For now, I close my eyes and let the warmth and comfort of his body lull me to sleep.

———

"Let's get our last date over with," I tell Sergey the next night after avoiding him whenever he's been in the apartment.

"We don't have to."

"No, that I did agree to and we'll do it. My choice, right?"

He nods. "Only if you're certain."

After a little bit of research and a change of clothes, I drive us to our destination. I want to drink my troubles away, even if only temporarily. Who knows if Sergey enjoys going to places like this, but I don't really care. The interior is dark, dimly lit, and the music is loud enough that talking obviously isn't the priority here. The bass hums through my veins.

I order myself a couple of shots and look over at Sergey.

"Water," he says.

"Oh no. I don't drink alone. Order something else."

He hesitates for a moment before conceding and ordering a beer. "Why did you pick this place?"

"To drink and dance."

My hand hangs in the air for a solid thirty seconds before he takes it. It doesn't seem as if Sergey is a fan of dancing, but too bad. He's coming with me onto the dance floor. While he may not be a fan, his hips seem to know what they're doing.

We spend the night dancing and drinking, avoiding talking as long as possible. This was supposed to help me forget. For the most part, it does. On the other hand, the alcohol and the closeness of our bodies makes me extremely hot and bothered. It steadily becomes harder and harder to handle. His hips seem glued to mine, his hands roaming as they please. Sweat beads on my skin and my breath shortens; it's not the lack of air conditioning making me hot.

"Let's go," I finally say, unable to take it any more.

Sergey pays our tab and then drives us back to his apartment. The studio apartment seems way too small for the tension still buzzing between us. The fact that he's been a gentleman, giving me space after all that's happened, turns me on even more. I flick a glance over to him as he shuffles through his drawers. It's as if I can see every muscle on his body flexing with his movements. I can almost still feel his body against mine.

It's our last date. Why not make the most of it?

Without thinking too much about it, I shed my clothes. Sergey freezes when he turns and sees me.

"Galina," he says softly. "What are you doing?"

"Do you want to talk or end the night on a high note?"

It takes all of three seconds before he rips his shirt off, taking a step toward me. I meant what I said; we might as well enjoy tonight. It's entirely possible this is our last night together. We should make it a good one.

———

While Sergey is gone to the arena for some kind of preseason work, I grab some of my things and leave. Being here is too much still. For some reason, I'm still undecided on what to do. I'll hang at a local hotel until my mind doesn't feel so frazzled. My mind wages a war with itself. Yes, Sergey was young like I was, but I can't wrap my mind around why he would agree.

We were friends. Friends who fooled around a little, but it's not like we were at a point where we would have married on our own. We weren't even dating. All I've experienced over the last several years is because he said he would marry me. Had he said no, I bet our parents would have let it go.

Then again, they may not have. Or they would have found someone else to marry me. As if I can't find a husband on my own of whom they would approve.

What am I supposed to do now? Our three dates are over, so it's either stay or go. It shouldn't be a hard decision. This is my chance to get away and finally take over my life. Why haven't I demanded a divorce yet? Who knows what the consequences of that will be? Either way this goes, I lose.

Two days pass before I decide I need to stop stalling, stop running away, and return to Sergey's so we can get this over with. It's late; I'm almost hoping he's too tired and wants to push it off until tomorrow.

I knock on his door and a moment later he answers. He's on the phone and it takes me a moment to realize that he's talking to his mom. Maybe even both of our moms?

"We are finished. We aren't doing this anymore. You have tormented Galina enough over the years and it ends now. Leave her alone. If she wants to talk to either of you, she'll call. Don't under any circumstances reach out to her. Not unless someone has died or is dying. Understood?"

I take a seat on the couch, listening as he continues to berate our moms. He sounds pissed, but they don't seem to care. They keep protesting, it sounds like. I stare at him in awe. He's actually following through. He's standing up to them. He has my back. He's talking to them so I don't have to. It may actually work. His mom hasn't called me anymore, only mine.

Seeing him talk back to them, full of fury on my behalf, warms my heart and turns me on. I push those thoughts from my mind. I need to make a decision. Do I stay or go and end my misery once and for all? Is there even really a decision to make?

CHAPTER 9

SERGEY

I f it wasn't for the few clothes that remained, I would've thought Galina skipped town. Seeing her return is a relief, even after being aggravated by our mothers. She's staring at me, but I can't make out her expression. I'm both glad and sad that she's returned.

Her absence made me think and I came to a decision. What she'll do from here seems quite obvious. She's likely leaving soon. Why would she stay?

"Hey," she says softly when I hang up on our moms.

"Hey. I have something for you." Might as well get this over with. This is actually the best outcome. We can move on. I hand a manila envelope to Galina. "You are free now."

Inside are divorce papers. I didn't tell our mothers about this just yet, but I will. There's no need for her to carry that burden as well.

Galina is confused for a moment before pulling out the documents.

"I don't know what to say."

I take a seat next to her. Our time together hasn't been that bad, but it's not what she wants and not nearly what she deserves.

"You don't have to say anything. We'll get this finalized and then you are free to do whatever you want and see whoever you want. Our parents still won't bother you." They better not. Unable to help myself, I add, "And if you ever need anything, I'll still be here for you."

She lunges at me, throwing her arms around me. "Thank you, Sergey."

"When do you think you'll leave?" I ask.

Galina hesitates as she pulls away and suddenly seems nervous. I would have expected more jubilation. "Actually, I think I'll stay, if that's okay?"

My eyes widen. That was not what I expected to hear. "You want to stay?"

"Yeah. Stay and see what happens. If you're good with that?"

She wants to stay? The disbelief is almost overwhelming. "Are you sure? This is your ticket." I grab the papers and wave them. She's free to go. She's free to make whatever choices she wants. "You're free to do whatever," I remind her. "You can be happy now."

"I know. Thank you; I truly appreciate what you have done for me and honestly, I wish I would have reached out sooner. Maybe you're right and we should give us a fair chance. Without outside interference. Things have been good so far, right?"

This is unbelievable. "If you want to stay, I certainly won't stop you." I've enjoyed having her around and spending time with her. It will be nice to continue that and get to know her better.

She opens my nightstand drawer and tosses the papers in there. "Let's table that then. Start with a clean slate. We can decide later if we actually want to be husband and wife."

"Whatever you want," I tell her, and I mean it. I've always hoped we would work out, and it looks like we're at the beginning of discovering if we will. She's had it much harder than I have and it's time things get easier for her. Whatever she wants, she can have. It's just more of that all or something mindset. We finally get to work on the something and maybe one day, we'll have it all.

———

JULY

"Ah, this is the life, Sergey," Galina says with a sigh. She glances over me, but her eyes are hidden behind a pair of sunglasses. Her smile, however, shines my way. "We should do this every year."

We're on a beach, the hot sun warming our skin. We've been here for two weeks so far and will be leaving soon. Things have been going extremely well for us. Going on dates while I'm home or enjoying time at home, whichever Galina and I are in the mood for. Our relationship has grown uninhibited. There's a vast distance between us and our parents, but the distance has been good for both of us. Each of our parents are learning how to respect the boundaries I've put in place that Galina has longed for all these years.

"Already planning a future with me, Galina?" I ask.

She laughs. "As long as it includes a vacation like this every year, absolutely." She rolls over. "Lotion me up again."

I throw my legs over the side of the chair, grab the sunscreen, and begin rubbing it on her skin. It's been one of my favorite things to do on this trip.

Galina releases another contented sigh. "I love you, you know?"

Her words make me pause briefly. She said it first about two months ago. It blows me away every time. I've worked so hard to get to this place with Galina and I can't believe she's rewarded me with her love.

"I know," I reply. She raises an eyebrow at me, so I add, "I love you too."

Another gorgeous smile. "I have a present for you."

"What's that?" I ask as I finish rubbing sunscreen down her back and legs.

"Look in my bag." Her bag rests between our two chairs. She sits up, crosses her legs, and waits. "Go on."

I shuffle through her things until I find a jewelry box. With a wary glance at her, I hold it between us. Wordlessly, Galina holds out her left hand.

"Put it on me, Sergey. Make me your wife."

"You're already my wife."

She laughs. "But I want to actually be your wife."

I don't believe her. That would be news too good to be true. "Are you sure? Don't you want me to propose? To have a wedding?"

Galina shakes her head. "One wedding was enough and I don't want you to ask. This is my decision." Uncertainty causes her hand to lower to her knee and her shoulders to slump. "Unless you don't want to? We don't have to change anything."

I open the ring box and take her hand. With a steady hand, I slide the ring onto her finger. "I would love to have you as my wife." The moment her ring is in place, she leans forward to kiss me. Her fingers tickle the back of my neck and I pull away just a little before I realize what she's doing.

She lets my ring fall into her hand. "Your turn," she mutters as she slips it onto my finger and lets the chain fall into her bag. "I know nothing is actually changing, but it feels different, doesn't it?"

It does. It feels more real this time. Both of us are actually making a decision for ourselves. The time that I've had with her since she decided to stay has been nothing short of amazing. It hasn't been pretty, but it's been us figuring each other out and learning more about one another all by ourselves.

Galina seems like a new person. The expectations each of our parents had for her clearly weighed her down. She's as light as a feather these days. That's one reason I wanted us to take this vacation together. It's been up and down as we navigate our separate routines and having two solid weeks with nothing to do but enjoy ourselves was much needed.

A server walks by and Galina flags him down to order more drinks. There's something I feel like she has the right to know, but I really don't want to bring it up to her.

"What is it?" Galina asks, as if she can read my mind.

While Galina hasn't spoken to her mom, I have. She decided to start keeping tabs on us again after she found out Galina came to see me. And since she can't talk to Galina, she talks to me. Surprisingly, both of our moms have followed what I demanded and don't call us; granted, it took about two months before they realized I was serious. Once they knew I wasn't playing around, they started waiting for me to call them and I do so about once a month.

Last month, though, Galina's mom made a request. I've been sitting on this request for what feels like forever. I know what decision I want to make, but part of me feels as if Galina should decide instead.

"Sergey?" she asks, resting a hand on my knee.

The server buys me a few more seconds as he drops off our drinks.

Clearing my throat, I get it over with. "Your mom would like for us to visit."

Immediately, she frowns and her brows pinch together. "No." As if she feels the need to explain herself to me, she continues, "I don't feel ready for that yet. It'll be my luck that we'll go and she takes that as the green light to start up again, asking when there will be a baby. I'm not going, even knowing you'd come with me." Her shoulders drop a bit. "I do miss her though." Galina sighs as if the weight is creeping back onto her shoulders.

"Maybe next time I call, you can talk to her? Work on repairing the bridge between you."

"Maybe." Galina settles back into her seat with her face toward the sky. That's the only sign I need to know the conversation is over for now. I'm perfectly okay with it.

As I settle back into my own chair, I ask, "The team will be getting together in a couple months to reunite basically. Want to go with me?"

While I made Galina go with me to a few gatherings, I haven't immersed her in my hockey life too much. I've been more focused on dating Galina than anything else.

"I think it would be nice to get to know your friends a little better," she says, causing me to smile. "We should probably do dinner with Scotty and his wife too. She will be thrilled that we're wearing our rings." Galina pauses and then adds, "I'm sorry it took me so long to come directly to you to fix this mess."

"Maybe we had to be on separate paths before things would work. A few years of heartache in order to have a lifetime of happiness."

Galina turns her head and smiles. "You sound very certain of our future."

"I am." I don't know everything that is in our future, but I know there will always be an us. That's all that matters.

ACKNOWLEDGMENTS

Thank you, Kristalyn Thornock. You are always there to lend a helping hand and I appreciate you so much!

Thank you, Shannon Page. You are such a pleasure to work with and always do great work.

Thank you, Robin from Wicked by Design. You always deliver with my covers.

Thank you, reader. I'm excited about returning to the Carolina Rebels series after a hiatus and I hope you enjoy the story! Thank you for your continuous support.

ABOUT THE AUTHOR

 Lindsay Paige is a North Carolina author of multiple Young Adult, New Adult, and Sports romances. She also enjoys writing books with characters who deal with anxiety and depression, issues which are close to her heart.

If you would like to hear news before anyone else, interact with Lindsay, and have a place to discuss her books with fellow fans, join Lindsay's League on Facebook. Be sure to sign up for her newsletter as well or visit her website: www.lindsaypaige.com.

ALSO BY LINDSAY PAIGE

www.ingramcontent.com/pod-product-compliance
Lightning Source LLC
Chambersburg PA
CBHW071223170626

46809CB00005BA/1916